For Tiziana, as ever

First published in Great Britain in 2009 by Andersen Press Ltd, 20 Vauxhall Bridge Road, London SW1V 2SA.

Published in Australia by Random House Australia Pty., Level 3, 100 Pacific Highway, North Sydney, NSW 2060.

Copyright © John Bendall-Brunello, 2009.

The rights of John Bendall-Brunello to be identified as the author and illustrator of this work have been asserted by him in accordance with the Copyright, Designs and Patents Act, 1988.

Colour separated in Switzerland by Photolitho AG, Zurich. Printed and bound in Singapore by Tien Wah Press.

British Library Cataloguing in Publication Data available.

ISBN 978 1 84270 788 3 (hardback)
ISBN 978 1 84270 869 9 (paperback)

10 9 8 7 6 5 4 3 2 1

John Bendall-Brunello

Dinosnore!

ANDERSEN PRESS

push

pinch

snore snore snore

Come on, Mum, wake up!

elbow

snore

run

roll

slide

snore

swing jump

bounce

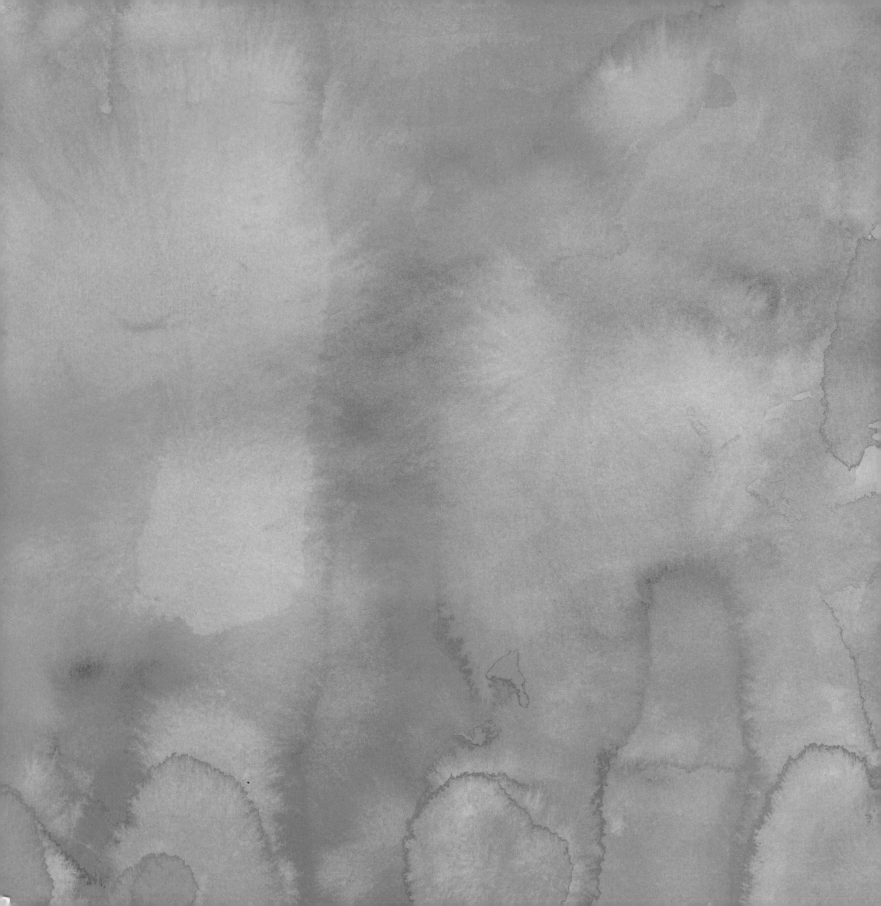

Other books you might enjoy:

I'm Coming to Get You!

Matty Takes Off!

Oops!

When Lulu Went to the Zoo

When Sheep Cannot Sleep